Angelina's
Sticker Book

Based on the text by Katharine Holabird and the illustrations by Helen Craig

PLEASANT COMPANY PUBLICATIONS ™

Practice makes perfect!

Dancing class is Angelina's favorite part of the day. She knows that she has to work very hard if she wants to become a world-famous ballerina.

Find stickers of two more dancers to fill the spaces.

The picnic party

Miss Lilly's dancing class is having a summer picnic, and the mouselings are looking forward to lunch. They've never seen such an enormous cheese pie. Angelina and Alice can't wait to try a slice!

Can you find stickers to fill the spaces at the picnic?

A lesson for Henry

Henry is to perform the Dance of the Sunbeams the very next day. Angelina shows him the more difficult steps, and little Henry tries hard to copy her. He so wants to be a graceful dancer, just like Angelina.

Can you spot the stickers that would complete this picture?

Dance of the Sunbeams

Angelina, Henry, and the other mouselings perform the Dance of the Sunbeams perfectly. Madame Zizi is proud of them all as they end the dance in a beautiful pose.

Find the stickers to complete the performance.

Mrs. Thimble's shop

While Miss Lilly chats with Mrs. Thimble, catching up on all the Chipping Cheddar news, Alice thinks about whether to spend her pocket money on some cheesy niblets or a delicious-looking lollipop.

Find stickers to fill the spaces in Mrs. Thimble's shop.

The bicycle ride

Angelina and Alice love exploring Mouseland on their bicycles. It's a beautiful day today, and they are off to the fields beyond the stream. Luckily, Alice has packed lots of cheesy niblets for the journey!

Who's missing?

To the stream

The Rose Fairy Princess

As Angelina soars through the air, the audience gasps with delight. Her classmates dance their hearts out, the orchestra plays the most beautiful music, and Angelina feels like the happiest princess ever!

Find the stickers to complete this magical scene.

Angelina takes a bow

At the end of a perfect performance,
Angelina curtsies beautifully.

Where is Angelina?